Bess the Barn
Stands Strong

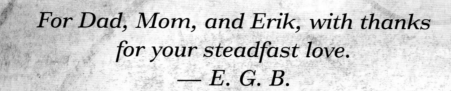

For Dad, Mom, and Erik, with thanks
for your steadfast love.
— E. G. B.

For Betty, Doefe, Sunny, and Maggie.
The best companions and feet warmers.
— K. H.

Text copyright © 2020 Elizabeth Gilbert Bedia. Illustrations copyright © 2020 Katie Hickey. First published in 2020 by Page Street Kids, an imprint of Page Street Publishing Co., 27 Congress Street, Suite 105, Salem, MA 01970, www.pagestreetpublishing.com. All rights reserved.
No part of this book may be reproduced or used, in any form or by any means, electronic or mechanical, without prior permission in writing from the publisher.
Distributed by Macmillan, sales in Canada by The Canadian Manda Group. ISBN-13: 978-1-62414-980-1. ISBN-10: 1-62414-980-4. CIP data for this book is available from the Library of Congress. This book was typeset in HK Carta. The illustrations were done in pencil, crayon, and gouache, and assembled digitally.
Printed and bound in Shenzhen, Guangdong, China.
20 21 22 23 24 CCO 5 4 3 2 1

Bess the Barn Stands Strong

Elizabeth Gilbert Bedia   illustrated by Katie Hickey

PAGE STREET KIDS

On a sunny June morning with the dew still sparkling on the prairie grass, they raised her roof.

Beam by beam and board by board, she was measured, hewed, and joined together by able hands.

She was steadfast. Sturdy. Strong.

The farmer named her Bess and held a celebration in her honor.

Bess loved the celebration.

Early the next morning, Bess flung her hearty doors open wide to welcome the animals.

A little shy and uncertain, the cows warmed
to Bess's sweet song made by the breeze
humming through her strong boards.

A mama cat and her kittens—one, two, three—
joined them after lunchtime to nap in the warm
sun spilling through Bess's gleaming windows.

At nightfall, long after the dinner bell, Bess spotted
an old barn owl lingering outside. She welcomed
him to roost on her sturdy beams.

As young and old nestled in, Bess's song drifted throughout her steadfast walls, letting each of the animals know they were safe and sound.

Bess's heart was full.

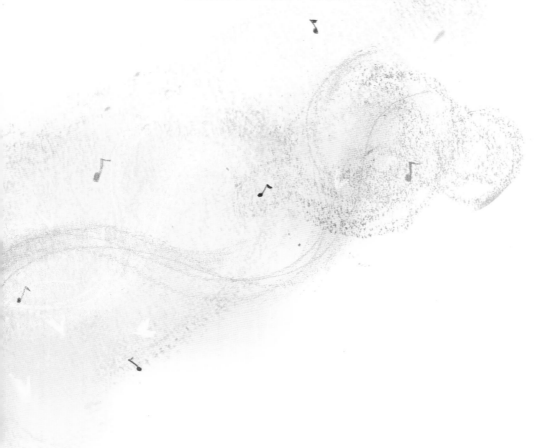

Bess was there for every celebration on the farm.

She saw life born into the world,
   struggling to stand,
      romping out to the pasture,

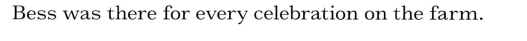

and life well lived leaving the world.

Fall was Bess's favorite time to celebrate on the farm. Twinkling lights were strung from her strong rafters. Hay was swept from her weathered wood floor.

Everyone gathered within her cozy walls to enjoy a harvest feast, hot apple cider, and a rollicking barn dance.

"Thanks for the evening, Bess," said the farmer, patting her side.

CIDER

Year after year, more celebrations went by with every season—from luminaries lighting the winter nights to the arrival of newborn animals in the spring to family gatherings in the summer sun to harvest time each fall.

Bess savored every moment, even as she and the farmer both became worn around the edges.

Then it was time for another celebration—
this time for a gentle farmer's life well lived.

The farm was sold to a young, innovative farmer.
He had new everything: new ideas, new-fangled machines, and
quickly, he built a shiny new barn for the animals.

It was all work now.
No time for celebrations.
No time for Bess.

Every morning, Bess watched the animals romp and play in the pasture far away. And every evening, the animals headed for their shiny new barn. Their new home.

Bess felt empty.
She sagged,
creaked,
and slumped.

Then one day, Bess saw a sky she had seen before—mean and pea-soup green. She knew danger was on its way. She shook off the cobwebs and dust and scowled at the angry sky.

Bess watched the animals dart and dash toward
the shiny new barn.

But the storm arrived first.

The roof?
Torn off and scattered.

The sides?
Tattered and split.

The beams?
Toppled and shredded.

Battered, but still standing, Bess knew what she had
to do. She still had strong rafters, sturdy walls, and
a roof raised with steadfast love.

She threw open her doors and in the animals ran.

Despite the howling winds outside,
Bess's sweet song drifted throughout
her walls, calming both young and old
as they nestled in what hay she had left.

Bess's heart was full again.

After the storm passed, Bess watched as the young farmer searched high and low for his animals.

Bess flung her doors open wide once again. All the animals had stayed safe and sound within Bess's walls.

"Bess, how can I ever thank you?" asked the young farmer, patting Bess's side.

The young farmer had an idea. One just right for Bess.

On a sunny June day right before the heat of summer set in, they raised her new roof. Underneath it were her same strong rafters.

New windows. Same sturdy hand-hewn beams.

A brand-new coat of paint. And the same steadfast, sweet-singing Bess.

Bess was ready to celebrate
for many more years to come.